MANGAL MEDIA

Evliya Çelebi Mah. Sadi Konuralp Cad. IKSV Vakfı
No:5 Iç Kapı no:2 Beyoğlu / Istanbul
Turkey

Writer
Efe Levent

Illustrations
generated by Efe Levent

Book Design
Feyza Daloglu & Efe Levent

Turtle Trainer, Efe Levent, 2024

ISBN 978-605-70348-7-8

TURTLE TRAINER

Efe Levent

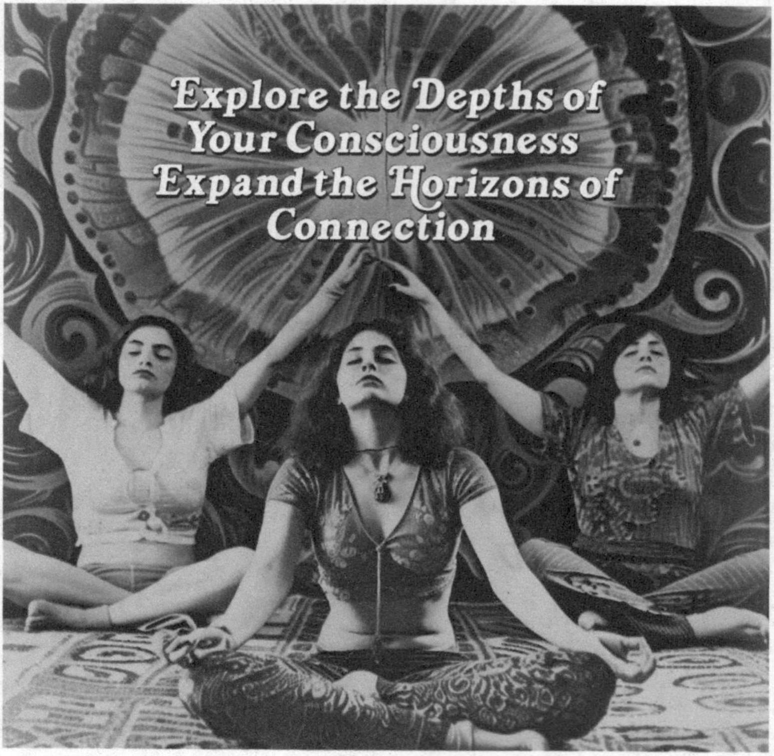

Explore the Depths of Your Consciousness Expand the Horizons of Connection

The Blue Lotus Society invites you on a journey of self-discovery and shared dreaming.

§ *Learn techniques of lucid dreaming, gaining agency within your own subconscious landscape.*

§ *Participate in guided dream circles, fostering a space of openness, acceptance, and shared experience.*

§ *Explore the transformative power of collective intention within the vibrant world of dreams.*

Awaken to a deeper understanding of yourself and your place within the interconnected whole.

Join us for a transformative Dreamwalking retreat at the **Blue Lotus Institute**: 45000 Albion Ridge Road, Albion, CA.

Editorial

Greetings dear readers.

1973 has been an eventful year for everyone. A war is raging in the Middle East, as I write this introduction for the delayed issue of the Blue Lotus magazine. It is a brutal war propagated by religious intolerance and fanaticism. It is in times like this that the work of the Blue Lotus society gains an increased significance to bring complete spiritual unity for all of humanity.

This year has been especially important to me. My journey of spiritual discovery across the world has brought me to a small village on the outskirts of Taizhong, in the island nation of Taiwan. To most in Europe and the US, the small nation means little besides the ubiquitous "made in Taiwan" tag branded on cheap mould injection plastic products. The handful of my fellow anthropologists who took an interest in this dynamic island nation have done so purely because they lack access to "China-proper". This being the case, there is a serious lack of engagement with Taiwan's unique culture and customs, particularly its indigenous communities. Leaving the privilege of discovering this island entirely up to me.

I write these words in a small mountain village inhabited by an indigenous community known as the Amis. Surrounded by thick layers of mist and rows upon rows of betel nut trees. The Amis practise a form of ritual collective dreaming that they refer to as "dreamwalking" which is the most fascinating form of spiritu-

al bonding I have ever experienced. Dreamwalking involves practising highly specialised meditational techniques while falling asleep, to open your mind to members of your community. This allows the entire community to share the same dream, each as if it were their own. While their methods for reaching collective enlightenment remain predictably primitive, the results they achieve are astounding.

I have experimented with many methods of merging consciousness. But none has been more thorough than the unity I have experienced with a group of village elders who don't even speak the same language as I do. As we opened our dream worlds to each other I felt the core of my personality expose itself as a mere facade. As the shell of my spiritual walls dissolved brick by brick, I learned that all the previous ego deaths I had experienced were an illusion. The humility I felt swell inside my chest was by far the most liberating sensation I have ever experienced.

As I have pointed out above, the methods of the Amis in applying their technique is very limited. With contemporary psychedelics we have access to in the modern West, we can accelerate dreamwalking to reach unprecedented depths within the human soul. I have also found their lack of interest in publicising and spreading their experiences to be uncharitable and frustrating. No matter how many times I tried to explain to the elders that their spiritual practices can be the ointment humanity needs to wrap its wounds. However, they remained sceptical about joining my efforts to develop new methods to teach and spread dreamwalking all over the world. As tribal people who remained isolated until very recently, they are suspicious of the outside world penetrating their dreams and fundamentally altering their identity. They simply fail to understand that the only way humanity can survive is through abandoning all artificial identities and binding ourselves closer through spiritual threads until our hopes, fears and dreams fuse for eternity.

The practice of dreamwalking among certain Amis communities is often compared to similar experiences that are connected to an artefact known as The Eye of Every Storm, located on this same island, in a museum in Taipei. The Eye of Every Storm was originally excavated in Anyang in the early 1900s when archaeologists discovered a series of oracle bones from the Shang dynasty (1600 BC- 1045 BC). These oracle bones are the earliest template for contemporary Chinese characters and have tremendous cultural value. But seldom mentioned among the discoveries of Anyang is a twelve-sided obsidian cube.

The foundational text of Chinese medicine known as **Huangdi Neijing**, (The Inner Canon of the Yellow Emperor/Esoteric Scripture of the Yellow Emperor) contains the earliest known reference to this dodecahedron. It names the artefact "The Eye of Every Storm" for its ability to connect various dreams into one and possibly to warn of the dangers that could ensue. The artefact wasn't brought to Taiwan until the 1940s when Chiang Kai-shek retreated from the mainland after being defeated by the communists during the Chinese Civil War. The Amis who have been dreamwalking for hundreds of generations claim no knowledge of the artefact, but it seems like a peculiar coincidence that the artefact has landed on the same island with the only people in the world who are naturally capable of reproducing its powers.

I will not speculate any further on the nature of the artefact. Such matters will require a great deal of further study. But I am excited to announce that this month's story has coincided serendipitously with my research on the Eye of Every Storm. It is a submission from Efe Levent in Turkey who appears to be as fascinated as I am with dreamwalking. The text makes explicit references to the mysterious artefact and can be read as a warning against using its powers to create an authoritarian society.

I am also a firm believer in threading with care around the unification of human consciousness. Techniques like dreamwalking and powerful artefacts like The Eye of Every Storm can indeed turn into terrifying weapons when in the wrong hands. Blue Lotus Society exists to bring about new ways of merging human consciousness under a unified religious system. But we also exist to make sure we are the right kinds of responsible people to bring about such a huge wave. One of the crucial ways to bring about this change in ourselves is for each one of us to experience our personal ego-deaths at least once. The other is to devote an important amount of energy into imagining possible scenarios in which the merging of consciousness has indeed become possible. We are fully aware that unawakened outsiders mock our attempts to capture the future through the medium of literature. But we believe that there is no better medium than the monthly science fiction magazine you are holding in your hands to prepare our miserable species for future scenarios.

Without further ado, buckle your space shuttle seat belts for a long and arduous journey to Mars with this month's story: **The Turtle Trainer** by Efe Levent.

Ellen Waltz

Turtle Trainer

by Efe Levent

Hürmet stood alone inside the empty meeting room, the lines on his brow contorted into knots as he looked down on the blinking red light from the document conveyor signalling a resounding failure. The room was an ocean of white, save for the spotless surface of the large blackboard. Four white desks were aligned meticulously under the bright fluorescent glow emanating from the ceiling. There was a heavy smell of disinfectant in the air. Hürmet had taken the duty of cleaning the station, he always took to it with much more enthusiasm than any of his brothers. He glanced around the room once more to distract himself from the problem with the document conveyor and surveyed his surroundings with a sense of accomplishment. The sense of order he saw around him gave him great comfort. They could be sitting atop a volatile geothermal cave on the surface of Mars dealing with countless uncertainties but at least standing on the sparkling white floors of the station he felt a sense of control. At least he was doing one thing right.

Instructions for the morning should have arrived by now. It wasn't at all like the central command to be so late. Hürmet couldn't stop thinking about what he had done wrong. All the technical maintenance in the base was the responsibility of his brother Hikmet who was adamant that both the conveyor and transmission tower outside were working exactly as they should. But could he have been wrong? If his excessively logical brother had at all been offended by the questioning, he certainly did not show it. He simply adjusted his thick glasses over his beady eyes and said: "I understand you are anxious, but you are being irrational."

Hürmet looked out of the window in vain toward the direction where the transmission tower was supposed to be, knowing fully well that he wouldn't see anything. They were a month deep into a global dust storm. Grains of sand were constantly pummelling against the station, a loud rasp perpetually grated against their ears. He hissed a curse word through gritted teeth, his palm sliding down his face in desperation. He had a habit of covering his face while expressing rage, almost as if he was too embarrassed to look at himself. Were he human, he would have been blushing right now. He glanced at his scaly fern-green skin with revulsion. What if he had warm blood? Or a supple skin that allowed complex facial expressions? He often thought his leadership position among his brothers was due to his compulsion to make himself more human. Humans were just much more compelling than he and his brothers could ever be.

He always had a keen eye for imitating human gestures. At first, involuntarily, almost out of reflex. But gradually, with increasing accuracy. As he grew old enough to understand what each gesture meant, his mannerisms acquired an uncanny meticulousness. Disappointment was a gesture he learned to perform early on. Perhaps even before he fully understood the sentiment it corresponded to. Most likely because this feeling was the first one that was conveyed to him. Just like their custodians, Hürmet expressed disappointment with a very elaborate ceremony. First, he closed his eyes. Then he turned his face sideways in slow motion as if peeling his face from a gory sight. Finally, he took a deep breath and deflated his lungs with a loud sigh. This gesture was but one colour in his emotional palette. He was an expert at using a wide range of such colours to paint sophisticated landscapes designed to influence the mood of his brothers whenever he needed to. He mixed guilt and passion, trust and calm, fury and pride so masterfully that they all seemed inseparable from each other. When he was with his brothers, he had a massive collection of signature shades and hues at his fingertips. But when alone, he never truly knew how he felt. So he defaulted to what felt easiest: disappointment.

Disappointment was what he was feeling in that bleached white meeting room with his hand covering his face. They were given a hero's send-off four years ago when they embarked on the *Bandırma* space vessel. A vast choir of children sang the *March of Youth* as if from a single voice and released hundreds of thousands of red balloons into the sky. The bright May sky choked with balloons, each one burdened with the expectations of a nation sending its first-born purebred mutants to Mars. An unscheduled moment of silence sunk in as the sky darkened by countless red specks. The crowd stood perfectly still, petrified by the artificial cloud they cast over themselves. Aghast, their mouths opened wide like a chorus of statues about to sing a silent hymn to some dark deity. From the small platform by the space rocket, Hürmet looked at the frozen faces below. He swelled his chest and waved at them triumphantly like he always dreamt of doing. But no one waved back. That's when doubt sowed its first seeds into his foggy mind. The silent crowd was mesmerised by the lingering shadow they cast upon themselves. A rapturous cheer erupted as soon as the cloud of balloons dissipated to reveal the bright morning sky. An enormous tide of sound thundered darkly over Hürmet. He grabbed the railing to stay steady. His muscles tensed with the weight of expectations loaded upon him. Instinctively, he put on his brave mask for the cameras that were projecting his face onto the giant screen below. He felt a heavy weight on his shoulder and recognised Hiddet's breath booming in his ear with excitement:

"Whoa! They're cheering for us, brother!"

A knot tightened in his throat at that moment. He couldn't tell Hiddet how he felt. Still, it was good to feel his brother lean against him

like a growing vine reaching for support. He felt sturdy, useful, needed.

Hiddet had a problem with authority since they first emerged from the breeding tanks. He had objected to this mission from the start. "Don't you realise?" He often yelled, throwing his arms in the air as if to surrender to everyone else's stupidity. "They don't love us. They say march: we march! They say die: we die!" When Hürmet insisted that they owe gratitude to the custodians for bringing them to this earth, Hiddet would snap back: "Easy for you to say. You're their pet!" Hürmet wanted to tell him of the countless times he saved his brothers ass. How each time Hiddet threw a stupid tantrum, he pleaded with the custodians to be more lenient with him. His delicate mind measured sentences to spit back at his brother but retreated when he saw the tempest brewing in his eyes. He caught a glimpse of the smooth, keratinous streams of scar tissue on his brother's shell and remembered how little he was able to do for him.

Hiddet carried these laceration marks like medals. Uneven notches marked the price he paid for being who he is. They tied him more intimately to the custodians than any of them. They were part of what shaped him into a super soldier, built of pure muscle and rage. Hiddet was what the custodians had intended to create. A savage beast they could unleash against anyone who would dare to threaten the nation's territorial integrity. His brother had fought for his station. While Hürmet simply grovelled for his.

As he stood over the malfunctioning document conveyor, he felt panic jolt through him from head to toe. Would he still be able to run the operations if instructions from Ankara were to cease altogether? He could already start to feel the morale of his three brothers eroding. Would he be able to keep them focused? The daily instructions may have been late for technical reasons, but what about his brothers? The expression of defiance in Hiddet's face flickered before his eyes. The way he tilted his head back and raised his chin, the way his eyes locked into a scowl, his heavy beak curled towards the right side of his face as if preparing to bite an intruder. Hürmet could see the animalistic nature they all shared bursting out of his brother to overpower his humanity.

Hürmet had been having the same violent nightmare ever since the dust storm first started. In the dream, He walked through an endless corridor lined with breeding tanks on both sides. They were exactly like the tanks they were raised in, with decals of a large blood-red circle with a white oak tree. At the end of the corridor was his short-tempered brother, writhing in pain on a throne of human skulls. His body was bruised and bloated. His gnarly voice muffled in pain. "I told you," he moaned. His fingers spasmed, his face contorted. Then his head jerked back and he let out a guttural howl in agony. His bloated body burst like a balloon. From his entrails, Hürmet saw hundreds of baby turtles crawl towards him... This is the point where he always woke up with cold chills.

He knew what humans called this sensation: goosebumps. To him and his brothers, it was a discomforting tingle on their carapace that Hayret had taken to calling "shell shock". He closed his eyes for a moment to chase away the intrusive thoughts. When he opened them again, the machine still gave no indication that it would ever work. Could it be that the file conveyor was beyond repair? Or heaven forbid, was there a problem back on Earth? The enemies of Turkey were many and they all had their eyes on the nation's Mars exploration program.

Just as he was running out of options, Hayret entered the briefing room. "Sorry I'm late" he said with his usual earnestness. Hürmet wiped off whatever expression he had on his face and painted a mask of righteous indignation in its place:

"Where have you been?"

Hayret scratched his head, unstartled. His brothers' moods washed over him like water off a turtle's back. His three brothers always took everything way too seriously! Particularly the custodians. The way Hürmet and Hiddet still competed for the custodians' affection made no sense to him. They were on another planet now, free to do as they pleased. None of the custodians had any clue about the upgrades Hayret had built in the kitchen to make a lahmacun oven. Even Hikmet, who initially considered his brothers' efforts to be a suboptimal use of resources, finally conceded that the crispy sheets of flatbread, topped with a special plant-based protein of Hayret's invention, had a tremendous effect on morale. Hayret had an intuitive connection with life. He could simply feel the needs of the organisms around him. Not just his brothers' or humans, but every living being. He could tame wild animals by whispering to them. He could sense how much light, heat and water plants needed as if through sense of smell. This is why he was in charge of agricultural production. When Hürmet saw his otherwise carefree brother walk into the room with an uncharacteristic worry carved on his face, he knew there was something more important at stake than the morning briefing. When Hayret finally spoke, the gravity of the situation became clear:

"One of the corn stalks in the agricultural sector is acting weird."

"Acting weird?"

"Yes! At first, I thought it might be infected but it's not like any infection I have ever seen before. It's grown red lumps on its leaves, each one the size of a hazelnut."

Hürmet's shoulders slumped with defeat. How will he deal with an infection spreading among their crops without any assistance from Ankara? Noticing Hürmets deep sense of despair, Hayret gently laid a hand on his shoulder "Don't worry brother, it's only a single plant. I will run some tests and figure out what it is." Hürmet raised his mournful head and gave an appreciative nod. He wished for nothing more than to hug his brother but feared that such an atypical display of emotion would put his qualification to lead under even more suspicion. Hayret was the only one of his brothers who would welcome a gesture of intimacy. Even though the four brothers were all born at the same time, Hayret always felt like the youngest of them all. Something about his character made him almost immune to petty rivalries. So why was Hürmet struggling to show his affection for his good-natured brother? By the time he managed to raise his arm halfway, it was already too late. The document conveyor sprung back to life with a thud and a loud whir. They both turned to face the machine. Hürmets arm was awkwardly left in mid-air with nothing to suspend it but a palpable sense of regret. The sound from the document conveyor merged with the sandstorm to build up to a screeching crescendo.

Hiddet and Hikmet were at the geothermal caves underneath the station to collect water from the vast condensation nets they had stretched over the cave ceiling almost as soon as they arrived. Suddenly Hiddet accosted his brother with a series of difficult questions. Hikmet, who never backed down from an opportunity to prove his superior logic was displaying a performative serenity. Hiddet knew that extracting vocal outbursts of emotion from his brother was a losing battle. But he was also aware that his brother had not looked at his watch once during their conversation. Hiddet knew that every minute they were late to Hürmet's briefings was like a firm punch to his pompous brother's gut. If his dumbass brother wanted to believe everything he was told by those assholes he insisted on calling "the custodians" that was his choice. Hiddet was going to have none of that bullshit.

As for Hikmet, what the hell did he know anyway? For all his intelligence and so-called reason, he was completely incapable of thinking critically when it came to questioning authority. His calculating logic was like a liquid that would fit into whatever cup it was poured into. If only Hiddet himself had become their leader he could put his brother's intelligence into use to free themselves from the control of those tyrants in Ankara. As they walked briskly through the bending main corridor of the crescent-shaped station, Hiddet expressed his point once more: "There is something they are not telling us about this mission!" Hikmet adjusted his thick spectacles across his broad nose and said "Would you care to substantiate this claim?"

Hiddet's temper flared "How about their treatment of us?" He was seeing red now. "Don't you remember how they beat us for failing their bullshit tasks? How they confined us as punishment? How we were raised like that shitty lab was the entire world?" He stood still, his eyes glowing with pure rage. The jerry cans in his hands were the only thing keeping his arms from flailing around uncontrollably. His legs stopped moving. He was slowly being drowned in a swamp of his own wrath. His nostrils flared like a bull, his breathing intensified. It took Hikmet a moment to realise he left his brother behind. His eyes rolled back wearily when he saw him heaving off his nose, transfixed with fury. "Oh, I know where this is going..." Hikmet said, shrugging behind the jerry cans he was grappling with both arms. He had a smug look on his face, proving his point was all he cared about.

"Oh my god!" Hiddet bellowed, fuming with rage. He could almost feel the sandstorm's permanent scraping in his skull. "This has nothing to do with that!" He growled with a menacing grimace. His rage was a cry for help. His eyes were glued to his brother with a desperate plea to be taken seriously. His attempts at sabotaging the morning briefing had come to bite him in the ass. He had planned to hit two birds with one stone by provoking Hikmet into giving an emotional reaction and frustrating Hürmet by showing up a couple of minutes late to his pompous pep talk. Instead, all he could think about now was the wound in his body where his penis was supposed to be. He could claim to be misunderstood, that his brothers always accused him of only caring about that one *thing*. But the truth was that he was understood all too well. He was burning with desires that he knew would never reach fulfilment. No amount of sabotaging his brothers would ever give him the satisfaction of feeling like a real man. Of feeling whole.

The so-called custodians had never made an effort to hide that their reproductive organs had been confiscated from them at an early age. Hiddet couldn't even remember the first time he was told about the peculiarity in his anatomy. He knew that a crucial part of him was missing for as far back as his memories stretched. His reaction to this absence hadn't just grown overnight. It had formed gradually, in layers. Like every child, they had asked how they came to this earth. The custodians had no time to waste with quaint stories about storks or mosque yards. But they couldn't tell them what they told their own children either: "When a man and a woman truly love each other..." Instead, they dropped the complicated reality on the brothers' laps and let them grapple with it. They showed them the breeding tanks where they were conceived and said: "we made you here." The rest of the conversation went more or less as follows:

"Were you made here too?"
"No."
"How were you made?"
"I was made by my mother and father."
"Where is my mother?"
"You are not like us."
"Can I become like you?"
"No."
"When I have children, will they be like me, or you?"

"You won't have children."
"Why?"
"Because that's how we made you."
"Why?"
"Because you have more important things to do than make children."
"What are they?"
"You will find out."

Hikmet walked into the starched-white meeting room, his space suit stained with the sludge and dirt from the geothermal caves. The loud whirring and clunking of the document conveyor harmonised mechanically with the chiming tools dangling all over his stained space suit. He dropped the jerry cans on the ground, not even noticing the squirming grimace on Hürmet's face and rested his hands on his waist as he looked around the room: "Wow ! It's squeaky clean!" he shouted to make himself heard over the chaotic chorus of the dust storm and the document conveyor combined. Hürmet's attention was fixed on the document emerging from the conveyor, but he had to express some form of resentment: "Yes!" He shouted back across the room "I cleaned it this morning." Oblivious to the hint,

Hikmet nodded in approval without saying a word. Not even when his brother rubbed his palm across his face nervously as he often did.

Hürmet hated the very thought of the caverns underneath the station. The heat source that made their existence possible on Mars was also a ticking time bomb. The hydrothermal vents in the cave were registering increased radiation levels. An alarming spike in radiation levels or an explosion from pressure buildup was a constant risk weighing on his mind. But not all disasters caused by the cave had to be so dramatic. A sudden rise in temperature or pressure could damage the equipment irreparably. Without access to the materials, it would be impossible to reconstruct them. Leading to a more protracted but ultimately, more agonising demise. After an entire year on Mars, they had finally recently started to install the sensors to monitor heat, radiation and pressure. Although it was almost impossible to locate all the heat and radiation sources inside the dark and hazardous cavities of the cave, they had to have as much control as they could. He was hoping the instructions from Ankara today would be about how to proceed with installing more survey equipment. He had become singularly fixated on knowing all there is to know about the caves without ever having to go there.

He would rather spend his time up here, in the civilised space station that he had nestled with great care. He was in a perpetual war against the fishy smell that percolated through the ventilation shafts and the sludge that his brothers brought. He knew he should really be grateful for the reliable volatility of the geysers below him. Having to depend on something so explosive and unpredictable troubled him greatly. What's more, their cold-blooded reptilian bodies were extremely dependent on external heat sources. His dependence on the geothermal cave below was a constant unwanted reminder of his reptilian blood. If this dust storm were to last much longer he would inevitably have to go into hibernation just like wild turtles. To do that, he would have to crawl down in the wet muck and into the warm protective belly of the boiling cave.

Just as he was thinking about the uncontrollable geysers underneath him, Hiddet entered the room. He had two jerry cans in each hand and a third one tucked under his armpit. He dropped them on the ground with a heavy thud and announced his arrival to the entire room: "So! Here we are!" Hürmet didn't raise his eyes from the conveyor, his expression was becoming increasingly confused. But not confused enough to forget his disappointment: "You are late."

Hikmet heard Hiddet's low growl behind his shoulder and raised his right hand to interrupt him. He approached Hürmet to make himself heard over the noise: "The sandstorm seems to have permeated the caverns somehow. I had to clean sand from the water filters before operating. I decided that hauling water should be prioritised over attendance." He said matter of factly, looking at the jerry cans on the floor. Finally relenting on his resentment, Hürmet acknowledged his pettiness: "You made the right call." The room fell silent for a moment save for the noise of the sandstorm grating against their ears. Even Hiddet, who had done whatever he could to start up a row since morning, quickly changed his tune. His eyes were bouncing back and forth between Hayret and Hürmet. The sombre look on Hayrets face alarmed him. He was not accustomed to seeing his brother like this. Something was not right, he could feel ancestral instincts clench his jaw and tense his muscles. His mind was denying the fear he was feeling but his body kept the score. "What's going on?" He finally asked with a shaky voice.

Hayret cleared his throat and scratched his head. He didn't want to alarm his brothers. Then he raised his voice to speak loud and clear:

"Well... one of the corn stalks has grown strange red lumps. I am trying to figure out what's causing it."

"Did you run tests on it?" Hikmet asked immediately.

"I only noticed it before coming to the briefing this morning."

Hiddet raised his voice impatiently to speak over the loud rumbling cacophony:

"Has the morning briefing arrived yet?" The second half of his sentence echoed across the room as the noises from the storm and the conveyor ceased abruptly at the exact same moment. The hazy twilight of the Martian sun crept through the windows to blend with the fluorescent lights overhead. Hürmet stood stunned facing the window, clutching onto the piece of paper that just emerged out of the conveyor.

A sharp darkness began to emerge through the sanguine mist. As the dust settled, a heavy dread sank through Hürmet's stomach. What had unveiled before him was an abyss so dark it devoured all light around it. A black dodecahedron chiselled with no instrument known on earth was defying the laws of gravity in front of his terrified eyes. It stood suspended in the air between the jagged rocks protruding out of the ochre Martian soil and the perpetual dullness of the Martian sun. Hürmet's mind warped around itself trying to conceive of its twelve sides. They seemed to be perfectly even, yet grossly asymmetrical at the same time. Each side was smooth as polished ice, emanating a reassuring darkness. Each side reflected the landscape in endless shades of dismal gloom. It stood here indifferent to the cosmic forces around it for longer than an eternity, pulsating a vast silence reminiscent of the moment between heartbeats. He took a step back from the window and lost his grip on the piece of paper he was holding.

Hikmet grabbed Ankara's instructions before they hit the vigilantly disinfected floor. A large dodecahedron was printed at the centre of the page. The black ink had sunk so deep into the paper, it felt soggy and crumpled. There was no trace of the meticulous instructions they used to receive daily from the HQ. Instead was a hastily handwritten command:

**LONG DUST STORM FORESEEN.
ACTIVATE HIBERNA-
TION MODE.
REPEAT:
ACTIVATE
HIBERNATION MODE.**

BROADCASTER: ONE NATION RADIO
PROGRAM TITLE: NEWS OF THE NATION
DATE: 23/09/2024
TOTAL RUN TIME: 10 mins 29 sec (as required by law)
ANCHORS: NISAN ATA, MURAT HILAL

ATA: Good evening loyal citizens across the four cor-
ners of our heavenly nation. You are listening to News
of the Nation on 88.2 One Nation Radio.

HILAL: We are coming to you live on the 23rd of Sep-
tember 2024, I am Murat Hilal.

ATA: I am Nisan Ata.

HILAL: And these are our headlines...

ATA: The ceremonial committee from Tunceli province
was greeted by the Eternal Başbuğ in Çankaya to celebrate the 86th anniversary of Tunceli's reunification
with the Turkish Republic. The ceremonial committee
performed their ritual of self-flagellation through
the streets of Ankara and had their customary dinner
at the Turkish Republic Ministry of National Unity to
celebrate the province's progress since its uncondi-
tional submission to the republic, following a misguided uprising in 1937 provoked by foreign agents.
The leader of the committee expressed his thanks on
behalf of the entire province for the generosity of
the Turkish Republic. Underlining that the people of
Tunceli are particularly grateful for the new veter-
inary clinics that have greatly increased livestock
yields.

HILAL: For the special occasion the Eternal Başbuğ
projected himself as a monumental pair of bronze hands
communicating in sign language, interpreted by famous
actor Davut Öztürk.

[Cut to voiceover]

"There is no better proof of the magnanimity of the
Turkish Republic than the acceptance of Tunceli back
into the fold 86 years ago on this day. No nation on

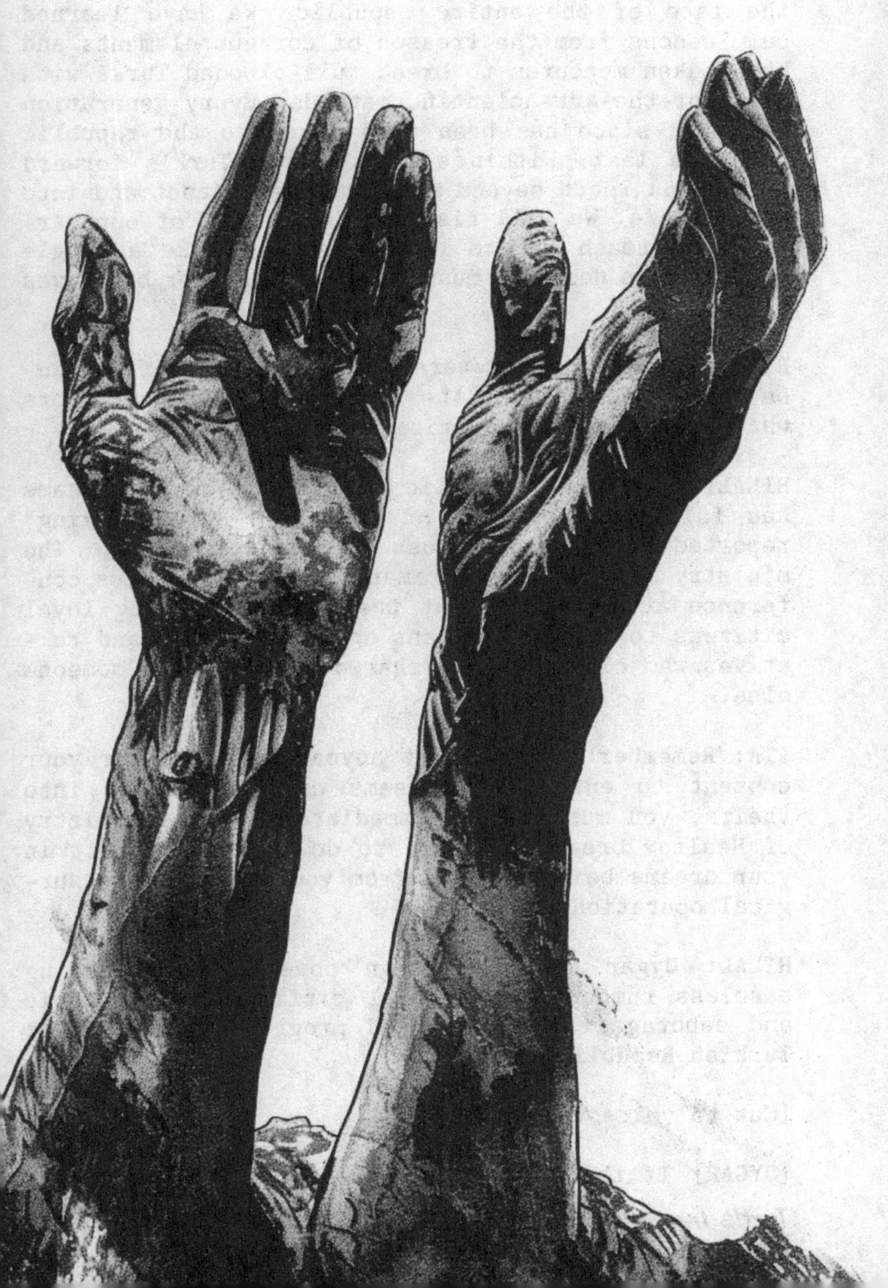

earth can tell us that Turks are a grudgeful race. We accept everyone as our brothers so long as they are willing to exclaim loudly: "Ne mutlu Türküm diyene." The events of 1938 have not only changed Tunceli but the fate of the entire republic. We have learned our lessons from the treason of corrupt elements and have taken measures to breed full-blooded Turks with state-of-the-art scientific methods. Every generation of Turks since has been more loyal to the republic than the last. Within a decade, the Turk's forward march will reach beyond this troubled planet and into outer space. We will rise from the blood of our martyrs and reach out to the red planet like a single body of pure flesh and muscle, bound together by nerves of steel!"

ATA: The celebrations were concluded by thirteen cannon shots to symbolise the thirteen thousand traitors who were neutralised during the uprising.

HILAL: The Turkish Republic Ministry of Healthy Dreams has falsified incidents of so-called "dreamwalking" reported by citizens across our heavenly nation. The ministry spokesperson Neriman Uygar held a press conference at 8 am today at the Ministry urging loyal citizens to remain vigilant against friends and relatives who claim to have shared a dream with someone else.

ATA: Remember: If you meet anyone who asks for your consent to enter your dreams or invites you into theirs, you must report immediately to the Ministry of Healthy Dreams. Failure to do so could result in your dreams being removed from your body with a surgical operation.

HILAL: Uygar blamed foreign powers for spreading baseless rumours among loyal citizens to sow panic and sabotage the light-speed progress of the great Turkish Republic.

[Cut to voiceover]

[UYGAR] If these incidents of so-called "dreamwalk-

ing" were indeed true, they would have been detected by our state-of-the-art equipment. We understand that our citizens' efforts to investigate incidents of "dreamwalking" may be well-meaning, but such rumours do nothing but play into the hands of foreign agents who are trying to divide our heavenly nation.
We are engaged in a perpetual state of war with the outside world to protect the integrity of our national soil. It is the duty of the Ministry of Healthy Dreams to maintain sanitary conditions for all our citizens so their dreams never conflict with our national sensitivities... The floor is now open for questions.

[REPORTER] I would like to take this opportunity to declare our gratitude to the Turkish Republic Ministry of Healthy Dreams for all the outstanding work they have done over the years to protect the nation from foreign agents who wish to divide it. Can you tell us about some of the Ministry's achievements since the hundredth year of our great republic?

[UYGAR] Certainly. Last year, on the hundredth year of our great republic we established ten new dream reprogramming centres with a total capacity of nineteen hundred and twenty-three beds. We also added twenty-nine dream monitoring vehicles to our fleet that can detect inappropriate dreams with unprecedented accuracy. We are looking forward to an eternity of safeguarding our national sensitivities under the guidance of our wise Eternal Başbuğ.

HILAL: And now for some happy news!

[CUE: MARCH OF THE YOUTH, GRADUALLY FADING OUT IN 10 SEC]

HILAL: Nisan, do you remember when we sent the four mutant turtles to explore Mars on May 19th 2023?

ATA: Yes! I do wonder what's become of them!

HILAL: You are going to love this! We have reports that they do in fact continue to be loyal to their motherland.

ATA: I suppose it goes to show that the blood of the Turk remains strong even in a low-atmosphere environment!

HILAL: That's right! The Turkish Republic Ministry of Science and Technology has issued a bulletin today to keep us informed about the situation of our shelled friends on the red planet.

ATA: I see you have brought some pictures!

HILAL: Can you tell our listeners what you are seeing in them?

ATA: Here is a picture of a Turtle climbing a giant transmission tower to raise an enormous Turkish flag. The picture is blurry, which one is this?

HILAL: Does it matter? Our cold-blooded brothers are casting the shadow of the Turkish flag over a distant planet!

ATA: Of course. Oh, what's the next one?

HILAL: Ah yes! Can you describe it to our listeners?

ATA: I see a corn plant with what looks like some kind of infection. It's a little gross... Why am I looking at this?

HILAL: Well that's the infection that was genetically coded into the corn seeds they took with them! Isn't that genius?

ATA: I don't...

HILAL: We have coded a genetic defect into their crops that can be remotely activated!

ATA: But...

HILAL: Please don't interrupt me. It's very disrespectful.

ATA: Sorry, I...

HILAL: This way, we can activate the infection in each corn stalk whenever we want. We can test their loyalty to our motherland by seeing how they will respond to the stress of a partial or a total crop failure. You would be more impressed if you could comprehend the amount of biotechnological expertise it takes to engineer a remote-operated genetic time bomb. Don't you see the brilliance of that?

ATA: I suppose...

HILAL: Because how else are we going to test the loyalty of our mutants, unless we put them through stress tests? Sure it's easy to be loyal to your country when your belly is full. But if you truly love your nation you will do so when the going gets tough!

ATA: Naturally...

HILAL: Looks like this is all we have time for today! Coming up next is a brand new episode of Lonely Mansion.

ATA: The Lonely Mansion is the story of four invalid brothers who return to their family estate in Eskişehir after fighting in the First World War. Only to find that their peaceful rural community has been hollowed out by the brutal Greek invasion. Things come to a boiling point in this episode as the four grieving brothers come home after their father's funeral and discover that their rifles are missing.

HILAL: See you at our next news bulletin at the same time tomorrow. Stay breezy.

ATA: Stay loyal.

"**W**here do you think you're going?" Hürmet called out to his short-tempered brother as he was strapping on his equipment and weaponry.

"Oh, you haven't noticed?" Hiddet snapped back with biting vitriol. "There is a huge black rock hanging in the sky?"

"You see a black rock in the sky and your first reaction is to run to it, like a moth to flame?"

"How foolish of me! Let's hear your idea. Oh wait let me guess. Does it involve taking a long cosy nap?"

A guttural howl emerged from Hürmet's belly. This wasn't the first time he considered taking on his brother in a fight. A glimmer of satisfaction emerged on Hiddet's scarred face. As far as he was concerned he had already won. He beat his leathery fists on his carapaced chest. His body's natural armour thundered like a war drum, amplified by the cavity of his distorted human ribs.

"Is that anger you are feeling brother? If You want me to obey the orders of the custodians, why don't you come here and make me."

Hürmet's fist clenched almost involuntarily. His vision focused on his brother, his mind sharpened into a lethal weapon. Then he heard a voice.

"Stop this at once!"

Hikmet stepped between the two brothers, his arms crossed over his chest defensively. His brow furrowed with the frustration of stepping between an irresistible force and an immovable object. His own deeply buried rage was starting to come to the surface now. He had it with his brothers' fight for leadership. He had it with them treating him as an impartial referee as if it were some great honour. Perhaps he settled into that role too comfortably. By siding with one brother over the other, he could earn a boost of respect and attention that he could then trade with the other for perhaps an even greater reward. He wasn't just angry at his brothers for relegating him to the sidelines. He was angry with himself for ever accepting that role. He had something to say now and he had to reach deep within his own well to amplify his voice.

"Listen. We are facing the threat of a crop failure, instructions that conflict with reality and that..." He hesitated, pointing out the window. They already had enough problems as it is, maybe not acknowledging the giant rock in the sky would have made things easier, more manageable. He could at least avoid defining what it is. "I can't believe all you guys think about is fighting."

Hiddet and Hürmet blinked with confusion as though waking up from a tormented dream. Their guards dropped slowly and they turned to their brother. Hikmet straightened his back: "Hibernation mode will reduce our food consumption and help the food stocks last longer. But if the infection spreads in the meantime we will be caught completely unaware."

A look of triumph glowed on Hiddet's face. Having Hikmet on his side had put wind in his sails. "But!"

His brother continued, startling Hiddet out of his glory. "We can't just blindly rush towards that thing either. We need to have a plan." He looked out the window again at the dodecahedron. It crackled silently, charging the twilit Martian sky with simmering sparks. It seemed to cover his body with a lamenting blanket of sound. The transmission tower outside had finally become visible and he found it impossible to get his eyes off it. He didn't remember it standing so tall. It seemed to stretch and extend like a sacred mountain into infinity. Its peak towered over rippling Martian clouds, with their shimmering wisps of ice crystals. His vision deepened, he saw vagrant coils of white noise spiralling the sky in search of a home. They crisscrossed acrobatically across the twilit Martian skies, shifting directions unexpectedly like those flocks of swallows he used to watch back home. Memories collided with each other in his nervous mind. Had he not done enough to maintain the umbilical cord that connected them to the motherland? Had he unwittingly severed his ties with the custodians by failing in the upkeep of the transmission tower? Was he now responsible for the misguided instructions, the mutiny brewing between his brothers?

His eyes opened wide, he saw the dodecahedron in the place of the transmission tower. He was transfixed. When he spoke, it was with a quiet raspy voice:

"It has a name."

His brothers looked at him with confusion. Silence and the overpowering smell of disinfectant filled the empty white room. Then he spoke once more:

"The Eye of Every Storm."

The Eye of Every Storm grew immeasurably as the space station and the transmission tower faded in the distance. New sensations overwhelmed me as I approached and my vision became crisper. Every time I looked up, it seemed to shift in unpredictable ways. The proportion of its sides changed in subtle but obvious ways. It bent the surrounding light unnaturally to create gruesome reflections. It throbbed with the quiet melody of endless lost memories, all coiled up tightly like hungry vipers.

This was the longest I had spent on the surface of Mars outside the space station. I had foreseen that the journey wouldn't be easy but was unprepared for how much attention it would take to constantly keep an eye on the suit's life support systems. I spent a good part of the morning walking across the Martian desert with my eyes transfixed on the HUD display, my mind devoured by an overwhelming sense of foreboding. For a long stretch of my journey, I almost forgot the nature of the endless, undefined abyss I was crawling towards. I ran countless scenarios in my mind of a dysfunction in the pressure regulator, a small tear in the outer layer causing a radiation leak, and a failure in the oxygen tanks. I knew exactly how excruciating death would be in each of these scenarios. However, obsessing over the gruesome details of my predictable demise helped me keep my mind off the terrors of an unknown one.

A biting cold weighed over me when I left the station early in the morning. As midday approached, temperatures rose to more comfortable levels. I switched off the climate regulator and allowed the solar panels enmeshed within the suit to soak up whatever they could from the faint Martian sun to recharge their batteries. I sat down for a brief rest to bask in the sun, aware of the possibility that this could be my last. On rare moments when the custodians graced us with free time, we would sit with my brothers under a lone tree overlooking the vast slopes of the Central Anatolian steppes. The landscape from my memories juxtaposed perfectly with the desolate copper canvas unfurling in front of me. How could this land be anything other than a product of my callous imagination? Gusts of dust devils spiralled furiously in the far distance, blazing a trail of spindrift in their way. The sand they scattered in the air descended unhurriedly in low gravity. This land was so erratic and violent, yet so deprived of life. These barren hills, this parched earth, but most of all these lifeless riverbeds. Like dead veins on rotten flesh, they branched out into twisted tentacles with nothing but ochre sand bleeding through their cracked lips. This land had seen water once, it had trickled through here with a gentle melody. Life once had a chance on this desolate red rock. But no more... This land was hard. Inviolable.

This brief moment of respite was the closest I had ever come to remembering how the sun used to feel against my scales. When all I could feel was the heavily layered fabric of the suit rubbing against the hardened scar tissue on my arms. I craned my neck to take a small sip through the plastic straw attached to my shell. Nutritional paste reached my tongue and coated it with a bland, viscous sludge. I felt grateful for the cold blood I inherited from my reptilian ancestors for making me unreliant on sustenance to warm my body.

I only noticed the length of the distance I crossed when I saw the shadow cast by The Eye of Every Storm creeping toward me under the faint midday sun. I stood up and checked all the systems once more. The fine Martian sand trampled under my feet. I refused to benefit from the low gravity on the planet to jump playfully over obstacles like some jubilant human child being taken to the playground by his parents. Instead, I threaded intently toward the source of the darkness as my turtle ancestors would. Lost in my reveries of the Martian landscape, I had forgotten why I had set out from the station in the first place.

Yes, of course, I had to see this giant rock that appeared suddenly after what seemed like an eternal dust storm. Of course, I could not obey the ridiculous orders coming from Ankara, telling us to have a little lie-down in the midst of a crisis. But aside from all that, I had to escape

Hürmet's dreadful domesticity. With his uptight rules and his unquestioning obedience. Hikmet and Hayret were more reasonable but excessively cautious. They tried to talk me into at least making a plan before I stormed out. But I told them they were just as chickenshit as the leader they chose for themselves. Now the transmission tower had turned into a faint line on the horizon and a sudden dust storm was all that stood between me and certain death, I questioned my judgement. I could always turn back. I could walk in through the airlock and tell them I had to cool off and was ready to hear them out. But instead, I kept walking. I spitefully savoured the thought of them staying back in their warm station to worry about the brother they shunned aside. I wanted them to tremble with fear, guilt and shame for not standing shoulder-to-shoulder with me when push came to shove. I wanted to punish them!

By the time I found myself right below The Eye of Every Storm, the already dim Martian sun was fading behind a

hill up ahead. Standing this close to it, it seemed every bit as mystifying yet somehow less frightening. The first thing I noticed was that the shape seemed to shift a lot less in closer proximity. It stayed stable for several minutes at once then only change ever so slightly when I looked away and back again. When I first laid eyes on it from the station, it seemed almost as though it was constantly in flux, like it was made from some sort of liquid material that defied human perception. Although it was a lot more stable up close, it seemed troubling in all sorts of other ways.

From the ghostly reflections on the rock's obsidian surface, I saw glimpses of memories I had buried so deep, I wasn't even sure they were mine. Rippling images in shades of black projected themselves to me on the dark glittering surface. I saw endless corridors of glass breeding vats with endemic Anatolian species entrapped within a clear gelatinous liquid. An Angora goat with two additional horns growing in place of its eyes, was doing somersaults in slow-motion

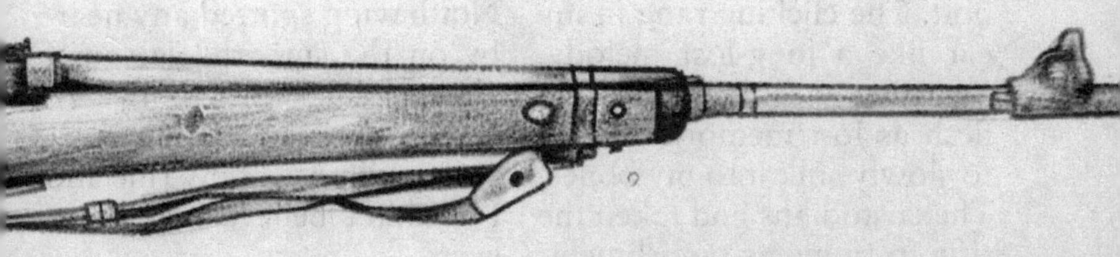

without moving its limbs. A Van cat with fangs as big as its head was floating belly up, paws stretched out as though jumping in mid-air like a ballerina. A Mediterranean Monk seal with multiple eyes like a spider and various insect limbs, each stunted at different stages of growth, was staring at me menacingly through the thick glass.

And then I saw the rifle. The one I was gifted by the custodians on my eighteenth birthday. An extremely well-kept, still operational Kırık-kale infantry rifle from the First World War. I knew this rifle intimately. I could feel the weight of its walnut stock leaning against my shoulder, the wood caressing my cheek. At the centre of my palm, I felt the cold metal from the round end of the bolt. The clicking rang in my ear like a long-lost melody. Yearning and rage boiled my flesh as lost memories began to slowly sink into my bones. The custodians had taken the rifle from me as punishment. I don't even remember what for. All I remember is the fury I had felt. Now as the rifle's ghostly image appeared in front of me on the polished surface of the Eye of Every

Storm, I knew that I had made the right decision to come here. It did not matter if a dust storm were to rise out of nowhere to separate me from my brothers at the station and my body was to rot like the dead rivers stretched out on the ochre sands of Mars. All I ever wanted was to die with my rifle like a true soldier. I had to reach out and touch the stone.

The Eye of Every Storm was levitating right above me at about five times my height. I tried a couple of desperate leaps in the air, counting on the low gravity to carry me close, but my heavy turtle body did not even come close. On the fourth or fifth try, I yielded to the impossibility of this method and looked around for some rocks to pile up and climb. Not having spotted any nearby on the smooth plateau, I glanced back at the Eye of Every Storm to catch a reassuring glimpse of my rifle and I couldn't believe my weary eyes.

The surface where the rifle had appeared a moment ago was replaced by an opening. It was as though the mysterious obsidian had sensed my yearning to reach for it and opened an orifice for me to walk through. I knew that this opportunity would only be temporary, it was going to disappear as soon as I looked elsewhere. I reached for the grappling hook coiled on my belt, without moving my eyes from the Eye of Every Storm. I spotted some runic carvings right around the mouth of the opening that the hook could settle and managed to secure it on my third throw. It was a short climb but the feeling of accomplishment as my feet touched the hard reflective surface of the rock was almost intoxicating. From the cavernous sound echoing through the darkness of the unlit corridor, I could sense that it was extending far far deeper than the external dimension of the rock would allow. I turned on the flash lamp attached to my helmet, only to be disheartened by the sight of an impossibly bottomless pit.

A prickle of excitement tickled the soles of my feet as I opened the maintenance hatch of the comms console and the machine willingly spilled its guts to me. Machines did not have unreasonable expectations, they didn't hold irrational grudges. They had the good sense to voluntarily submit to the sharp focus of my rational lens. They were solution-oriented and so was I. I felt a sense of warmth and security as I crawled deep into the viscera of cables and circuits, proud of the knowledge that I was the only one among my brothers who hadn't lost his mind amid the crisis. I was following standard operating procedures for repair and maintenance. Starting my inspection with the most accessible component and working my way down. If your engine doesn't work you have to check the fuel gauge before replacing the spark plug. It's as simple as that.

The knots of cables that greeted me inside the hatch were a disappointment. I remembered not having the time to organise the cables neatly when we were setting up in a rush, but I must have chosen to forget the exact state of disarray I had left them in. Although there were no obvious signs of a short circuit or loose contact. There was no way of being absolutely sure without tracing each wire by hand with heavy-duty rubber-insulating gloves. While I was down here, I decided the best thing I could do was to organise the cables like they were meant to: by proximity and colour code. I reached for a bundle of zip ties from my cargo pocket and set about bundling them neatly. The joy of having a well-defined and useful task thawed my cold reptilian blood. A sensation of purposeful comfort rippled through my shell.

Unlike my brother Hiddet who wandered out into the icy Martian dawn with no clear plan nor purpose, I was methodically advancing towards a rational and achievable goal. It's not that I had no sympathy with his plight. We were all scarred by what the custodians had called our "circumcision". But he was the only one among us who acted as though he could rewind the operation and be whole again. Needless to say, I found his obsession to be highly illogical. Why get so obsessed over aspects of your life you have no control over, when you can focus on goal-oriented tasks and change the circumstances that you **can** control?

Just like I am doing right now.

A loud gurgle of white noise from the console speakers suddenly interrupted my meditative routine. The machine I had been so meticulously trying to repair had unexpectedly come to life. Yet I felt more vexed than jubilant. I had done nothing to elicit this new development. I slid back out from the warm entrails of the console, frustrated about my unfinished work and browsed the blinking lights on the panel board. The signal indicators for the S-band and X-band frequencies used to communicate with Earth were off. Not even a red light to indicate the absence of a broadcast. But the VHF indicator glowed with an inviting green. It meant that there must be a broadcast right here on the surface of Mars. I reached for the dial but recoiled in shock as I noticed it turning by itself to locate the broadcast.

The voices hissed and garbled as the radio picked up various signals from different broadcasts. As I watched the dial turn sluggishly, I picked up words severed from their context by the *March of Youth:*

"*Mountain top covered in fog*...Have been apprehended at a... Bronze hands... *Silver stream flows endless*... Negotiating with terrorists... Ministry of Healthy Dreams... *The sun rising from the horizon*... Foreign agents... Nothing to worry... *Let every step make the ground tremble*..."

I stared at the console, my hands trembling with terror. My legs quivered as if shaken by a tectonic rumbling from the endless caverns beneath. I listened breathlessly as ghost broadcasts from home haunted the halls of the empty station. After a harrowing back and forth between patriotic broadcasts and the thundering void of static noise, the dial slowly ground to a halt. My entire body froze at the sound of the voice buzzing through the frazzled speakers:

"Lock, load, pull, release. Lock, load, pull, release. Lock, load, pull, release..."

I fought the urge to leap away from the console and grabbed hold of the microphone with an iron grip:

"Hiddet! Brother, can you hear me?"

"Lock, load, pull, release. Lock, load, pull, release..."

"Hiddet! Answer me!"

"Lock, load, pull, release. Lock, load, pull, release..."
I threw the microphone at the console with unbridled rage. All I wanted to do was crawl back into the warm comfort of the machine's underbelly and continue organising the cables as though nothing had happened. My brothers' voice was swallowing my conscience whole "Lock, load, pull, release." My fingers clutched desperately around the dial, but it refused to yield. Rage and fear were all that drove me. My vision blurred as I hammered the dial with my fist until my knuckles felt sore. My final punch must have been so hard, that the main-

tenance hatch swung open with a metallic screech. A web of gnarled organs gushed forth from beneath the console and spilled out onto the spotless white floors. My reptilian veins froze as I stared helplessly at the foul-smelling puddle of putrid blood crawling toward my feet. I stood bereft, unable to lift my eyes from the pulse of the living wires untangling around my feet. Just as I thought things couldn't get any worse...

A chilling gurgle of static emerged from the comms speaker to overpower my lost brother. His determined, mechanical voice gradually submerged under a tide of white noise: "Lock... Release... Load... Pull..." I reached for the dial, desperate to hear his voice again, no matter how disquieting. The dial yielded to my fingers yet there were no broadcasts for it to pick up. All I heard was the radio equivalent of the Martian dust storm I had grown accustomed to. The sound wrapped itself around the smell of decaying flesh like an unhelpful palate cleanser. I turned the dial slowly until the end, then all the way back again to hear Hiddet. But the giant lattice tower

outside picked up nothing but a monotonous blanket of radio static. The green light of the VHF was still glowing, my brothers' voice must still be broadcasting somewhere. The machine couldn't possibly be lying to me. My organic senses on the other hand were capable of falling prey to all kinds of cognitive biases. Perhaps, the voice of Hiddet that reverberated through the comms speaker was nothing but wish fulfilment. The lights on the console board, the garbled broadcasts from Ankara and most of all the squelching gore and viscera beneath my

feet were most likely figments of my deprived imagination. There was something I could do to find out. But I wasn't ready to face the possibility that my sanity was slipping through my hands. My trembling finger hesitated to obey my mind's command.

I suppressed my fear and hesitation for a brief moment and pressed the console's power button in one fell swoop. The lights on the console faded instantly. The sound from the speakers gradually faded, only to come back even louder as if seeking revenge. I hopelessly shielded my ears with both hands knowing it would be no help. The source of the sound was not the speakers anymore, it was my own mind. A cold sensation tickled my toes and crept up toward the sole of my right foot. I looked down and saw the harrowing sight I had been trying to forget. Only a few minutes ago there was nothing I wished more than to bury myself within the comforting depths of the console. But now, the rancid smell of rotting meat nestled itself at the back of my throat and made me retch. I held my breath and tore savagely at the guts, veins and nerves inside the console in a futile attempt to silence the radio. I even bit down on some of the more tenacious tendons with my powerful jaw, my sharp animal beak ravenous for destruction. I had submitted to the worst part of my nature. What the custodians used to call the "reptile brain".

By the time I came to my senses I was covered in dark putrid blood, bits of flesh and muscle tissue hung loose all over my uniform. The gnawing hiss of radio static was rustling incessantly inside my aching skull. I looked around in devastated agony for a solution or a sign to reveal itself. The room was in its usual state, oblivious to the tragedies of the organisms that occupied it. The world's cold indifference to my torment weighed down on me, I sank deeper and deeper into an impotent, cornered rage. The sensation of a gluey substance drying on my scaly cheeks alerted me that I must have been burying my face in my blood-stained palms. I leapt in revulsion at my state and found myself running around the room wailing helplessly, my vision blurred with beastly rage and fear. Like a morbid brush dipped in gore, I had been smearing the room in a dark veinous red. Perhaps I was painting the very sign that I was trying to find. Finally, I collapsed on the floor breathless. My trance state came to an unexpected end just as abruptly as it had started. I crouched by the window to catch my breath. White noise was still reverberating relentlessly in my skull.

When I raised my head, I saw the base of the transmission tower. The familiar sight gave me comfort. I had built this tower from scratch with my own hands. My eyes climbed slowly along the web of metallic veins, appreciating the sheer power of electricity pulsating within. About halfway through their journey to the top, my eyes spotted something impossible. A chilling sensation crawled across the back of my shell. First I blinked in surprise, and then a sharp gasp escaped my bloodied beak. Disbelief morphed into sheer terror as the realisation crashed through my bones.

The tower had grown.

I rushed to the window and craned my neck to see how far it had extended. If I could measure the distance between the former and the current peak, I could quantify the depth of my gradual descent into insanity. The tower now reached intently into the cold void like a colossal hand. I stood awed by its omnipotent strength to conquer cold silence by humming signals from near and far. The grating sound of white noise grew unbearably loud as my eyes finally reached the impossibly tall peak of the. An unnatural panic gnawed mercilessly at the back of my throat. I stood staring at the chilling absence atop the monolith. But this time I could feel my muscles twitch back to life with a true sense of purpose.

Where was the flag? The flag! The flag I had hung atop the tower when I had finished building it. My mind cleared and my vision focused. Why get so obsessed over aspects of your life you have no control over, when you can focus on goal-oriented tasks and change the circumstances that you **can** control?

Just like I am doing right now.

"**I** hate this" I muttered to myself as I put on my helmet to venture into the thermal caves below the station. Oxygen, heating and pressure systems lit up on my HUD. Hikmet's voice buzzed through the scratchy speakers within the helmet as soon as I put it on.

"Come in Rearing Horse, this is Mother Bee, do you copy?"

"Roger"

"Mad Dog is returning to base, says he has made some important discoveries."

"I bet he did. I'll come back up once I'm done here. Over"

"Let me know if you need backup. Over"

I sighed with relief at the thought of Hiddet returning from his ill-considered expedition to The Eye of Every Storm. Perhaps whatever he discovered out there helped him see some sense. Though frankly, I doubt it... The feeling of relief only lasted until the airlock opened to reveal the smouldering scenery of the dark cave. I had done everything in my power to avoid coming down here. But now here I was, doing what I could to fulfil orders from Ankara. We had built the hibernation chambers inside the cave to make sure it would be heated adequately. I was initially worried about nesting so close to the hot water geysers due to their unpredictable volatility, but Hikmet had insisted that if a large explosion were to occur

in the caves while we were hibernating above, we would simply die a slower and more painful death. He also wanted to make sure we had plenty of heating to eliminate the risk of hypothermia. Predictably, Hiddet was in full favour of this plan. Not because it was more rational, but because it was way more exciting to be blown to smithereens by an eruption of scalding water and sulphur than to quietly freeze to death in his sleep.

I begged to differ. Since we arrived on Mars, I often wondered what it must be like to gently drift out of consciousness and simply dream myself out of existence by following the light. These thoughts were particularly vivid in the mornings while I stood in an empty white room, waiting for the document conveyor to spit out the orders from Ankara. The same thought of a restful death was now coiling around my head as the damp heat of the cave began to form tiny droplets on the surface of my helmet. I took a deep breath, exhaled a quiet "Bismillah" and turned on my headlights.

With my first step into the cave, I felt the slippery basalt floor sliding under my heavy boots. I got fixated on the sharp cave formations reaching out to each other from the floor and ceiling. Some had succeeded in combining into sweaty chubs and morphed into natural columns. But most had failed. Stalactites and Stalagmites stretched out in eternal yearning to join hands with each other. Their mournful efforts filled me with such an-

guish. For a moment I felt I heard their wailing from the helmet speakers. I chased the thought from my mind in a rush. There were more pressing matters to attend to. A slip of the foot could cause a lethal fall straight into the cave's ferocious maw. I could land face down into a sharp molar protruding from the ground, my helmet breaking into pieces, a sharp rock piercing through my bloodied skull. Perhaps a heavy fall could even penetrate my solid shell. It could puncture a web of fractures through its keratinous surface, making a sickening crunching sound as it rends my flesh and crushes my bones.

The rock formations extended into terrifying shadows under the suit's headlights. They leaned and twisted aggressively, heavy droplets of ochre liquid dripped from their hungry jaws like saliva. All the heavy equipment we had set up here upon arrival was dwarfed by the cave's endless jagged teeth, formed gradually over millennia. Whether I liked it or not, this was the beating heart of our surface station. The wire condensation nets suspended on the ceiling to harvest vapour , the turbines whirling efficiently under the geysers; they pumped the water and electricity we needed to stay alive. After crossing the muddy floor where an underground water source had carried silt since time immemorial, I reached the hibernation chamber. As I approached, the bright halogen lamps detected my presence and lit up. The hibernation chamber glowed bright under the light's itense glare. It was everything I remembered it to be: a bulbous dome made of thick ballistic glass, equipped with some of the most high-tech equipment we had brought from Earth. I promptly set about to check if all systems were operational. Biometric scanners: check, automated waste management systems: check, thermal regulation equipment check. The control systems all glowed with bright emerald lights. The chamber was in perfect working order. Yet I had the peculiar feeling that something was not right.

"Mother Bee, this is Rearing Horse. Do you copy?"

My voice echoed helplessly through the rumbling bowels of the cave. I stood awkwardly for a moment that felt like an eternity, waiting for a response that refused to come.

"Mother Bee, this is Rearing Horse. Do you copy?"

Then I heard it...

Hikmet's voice rang from the other end of the connection in a muffled tinny hue. There was no hint of emotion or life in his voice:

"Brother finger, brother finger, where are you?"

"Mother Bee? Do you copy? Mother Bee!"

"Brother finger, brother finger, where are you?"

"What's going on up there?"

I heard a click from the other end followed by a high-pitched squealing sound. Startled, I called out once more. Not even expecting a reply:

"Mother Bee, Mother Bee! What's that sound?"

An orange text appeared on my HUD: "CAUTION! OXYGEN INTAKE INCREASE: 20%" I stood still for a moment concentrating on slowing my breathing. Just as I was about to remove the helmet to use the oxygen from the hibernation chamber I heard the squealing sound once more. My three-chambered heart was beating at a terrifying speed. Visions of a terrifying monster flashed in my mind. Perhaps something indigenous to the planet, or something sent to Mars by the enemies of Turkey to prevent us from claiming this planet on behalf of our country. Perhaps it had already claimed my brothers' life and the squealing sound was a blood smeared limb dismembered from one of them. This must have been why Ankara had ordered us to go into hibernation behind this impenetrable cage of heavy glass. I would surely be rewarded for my loyalty and resourcefulness once I get back to Earth. But first I had to get out of here alive. I clenched my fists tight and wished for the Eternal Başbuğ to grant me the power I needed. What I saw when I turned back was no immediate danger or threat, yet somehow far more harrowing.

A red balloon was whimsically brushing against the thick glass wall of the hibernation chamber, prodded gently by cavernous underground winds. I took a step toward it for a closer look. It was an ordinary party balloon filled with helium, completely out of place in a thermal cave on Mars. Its nonchalant cheeriness filled me with indignant rage, reaffirming my suspicion that I was the only one among my brothers taking this expedition seriously. Unbound by the expectations that weighed down upon me, the balloon scraped itself from the transparent surface of the glass wall and playfully drifted into the bruised innards of the cave. I turned on the radio and yelled angrily, not knowing who it was intended for; my brothers or the mischievous red balloon drifting buoyantly into untold danger:

"You guys need to stop fooling around!"

My shout was once more greeted by a heavy silence. Panic and fury were gulping down my oxygen supply. I had to take a rest here and fill my tanks if I wanted to journey into these unknown depths. The balloon was fading into obscurity outside the range of the violently bright halogen lamps above the chamber. I had to know where it was going. I rushed out. The veins in my temples were pumping blood in a savage rush. The closer I got to the balloon, the faster it seemed to get away from me. My oxygen bar was decreasing visibly as I threw caution to the wind and ran toward the balloon as fast as I could, oblivious to the slippery floor that terrified me only a short while ago. The rock formations and their ominous shadows jolted violently, under the bouncing light shining from my suit. Finally, I cornered the balloon leaning against the damp wall, floating airily next to a diagonal fissure. Narrow rivulets of turbid sulphur water were bleeding from the alabaster pores on the wall surface, all of them converging into larger streams haemorrhaging into the mouth of the large opening. As the light steadied and my vision focused, I noticed a fragile green thread precariously lining the mouth of the fissure. My eyes opened wide. Could this be... Life?

I pressed my finger on the edge of the fissure as gently

as I could, as if it were a fresh laceration mark on the ruddy skin of a delicate human in severe pain. The thick gloves of the space suit didn't make it easy to ascertain but I could feel that this was moss. Wherever this fissure was leading, there must be something living on the other side. Praise the Eternal Başbuğ! I would certainly be praised upon my arrival home for this discovery. I hauled myself gently into the fissure sliding through it gradually. I had never been so grateful to my turtle ancestry for allowing me to retract my limbs into my shell to slip through tight passages. After a few hours of advancing slowly, my lights began to flicker and a message appeared cautioning me that my oxygen level was reaching 35%. There was no way back now. The only way out was through. The thickening moss brushing luxuriantly against my space suit assured me that there would be plenty of air to breathe on the other side. My radio switched back on unexpectedly and I heard the voice of my three brothers sing in unison:

"Brother finger, brother finger, where are you"

I gulped anxiously. Pushing the knot in my throat down into my stomach and replied:

"Here I am, here I am, how do you do?"

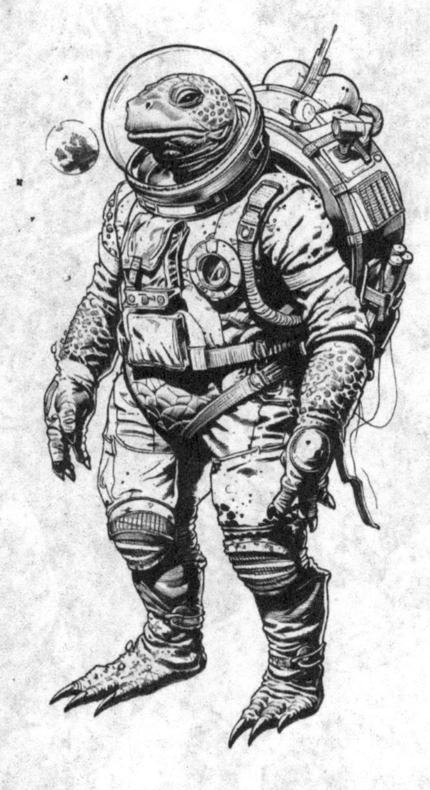

Unlike what my brothers seem to think, communing with nature is not something that can be done effortlessly. On the contrary, It takes tremendous amount of concentration and physical strength. The consequences of understanding the yearning and suffering of all life around me always took an unbearable toll on my wellbeing. My brothers' fury, anxiety and wilful denial often felt like hooks sinking into my flesh to tear me apart. All the more so because they mirrored my own fury, anxiety and wilful denial. Half the time I struggled to distinguish myself from them. The other half I was alone in my dreams, where the boundary between my consciousness and theirs was impenetrable.

Or so I thought...

I had barely stepped outside the agricultural sector since the appearance of The Eye of Every Storm. I didn't remember how long ago I came here. I knew I had to find the infected corn with the red lumps. But instead, I had been wandering through endless fibrous corridors, unable to find a way back or forth.

The more I walked among the stalks the taller they grew, until I could see nothing but an eternal curtain of green stems and leaves.

The rustling of the plants were helping me drown out the noises broadcasting from my brothers' tormented souls. I didn't know where they had gone, but they were yelling, mumbling, crooning and wailing as if they were right there with me. My thoughts fizzled and dipped into a cosmic abyss where reality frayed and withered. I was struggling to tell what was real and what was a product of my sleep deprived imagination. Too afraid to commit myself to unmooring completely, I floated precariously around familiar shores, staring yearningly at the dark waters extending into infinity.

Voracious green leaves swayed wildly around me and brushed against each other in the windless hall of the agricultural sector. They whooshed and swished loudly as if to grant me occasional moments of respite from my brothers' cryptic screeching. I turned my receivers to the soothing white noise of the

plants, as though desperately tuning in to a ghost radio station broadcasting static into the dead of night. The leaves wafted a peculiar odour as they wavered back and forth. A scent of rotting sweetness, like flowers blooming over the decayed carcass of an animal. At first I thought it must have been from the sticky sap oozing through the unnaturally thick stems. It was a partially translucent, mucus-like substance. Upon touching it, I realised it had a slightly irritant feel against the clawed, rugged scale on my fingertips. I brought it to my nose for a sniff, but found it to be odourless. The scent must have been from another source. Too bad turtles aren't known for their sense of smell.

I pushed and shoved my way through the stalks, occasionally bending or snapping them. They cracked with an unexpected roar and tumbled down like tropical trees, their broken stems oozing with the strange sap. After some time trying to find my way under the increasingly darkening canopy of the giant corn stalks, I noticed I was covered in the sticky substance. It felt like a thou-

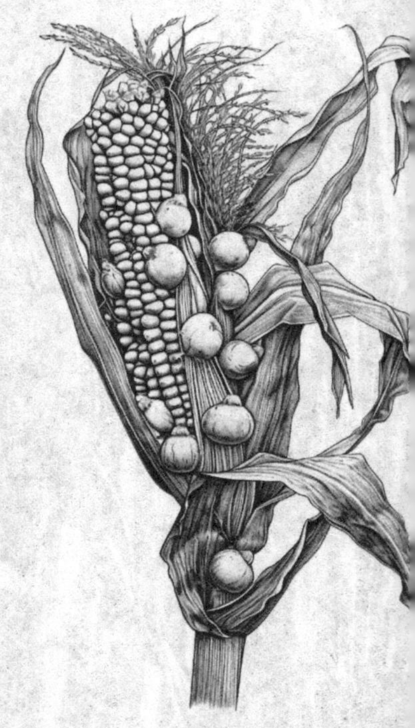

sand tiny insects were biting my flesh at the same time. I had to stop occasionally to scratch my hands and face. I took advantage of these moments to be grateful for not having soft pink skin like the custodians.

The smell seemed to intensify, the deeper I got lost within the maze. But I felt no closer to its source. My brothers' voices slowly faded to be replaced by the white noise from the bustling flora. At first, I felt relieved. Not having to sense my brothers' troubles felt like a weight lifting from my shoulders. I didn't have to take sides in their conflicts, nor salve their open wounds with empathy when they were throwing temper tantrums. They always reminded me that they saw me as their youngest, because I took a backseat during moments of conflict and decision making. I never had their bullheaded determination to decisions and principles. But though never spoken out loud, they also treated me like their eldest whenever they needed a compassionate eye to look through their rugged shells and see the hurt hatchlings beneath. But under the sunless shroud of the giant plants, I was all alone. Separated from my three tormented brothers who always argued about the best course of action. Now, I had no one to take responsibility for failure or success, in exchange for compassion. I took a big sniff and inhaled the sickly sweet smell. The scent reminded me of our memories together for one last time before their voices faded completely and got replaced by the white noise of the lush flora, which now seemed to move almost of its own volition...

The itching sensation on my scales pulsated along with the cadences of the rustling leaves. In the absence of a visible external force, they wavered and swept against each other with vicious hostility, as though they were battling each other for territory or resources. Occasionally, a particularly violent scuffle would break out among them at a distance I couldn't measure. I could hear the sharp whistling of the stems as they whipped the air and spiralled around their own axis with inscrutable determination. These conflicts rippled out in gnarly waves, making the stalks lean one way or another. With each pulsing of this mysterious jolt, I felt irritation sink into my flesh and reach deep into my bones, as if absorbed by osmosis. All my senses felt ambushed and assaulted. The noise, irritation and the horrid smell reached a climaxing crescendo. It was then that I heard his voice booming in my ear:

"Follow me child"

My heart pounded in my chest. My lungs sucked all the air around me in desperation, pumping themselves full for a terrorised howl.

"Wh… Who are you?"

"Patience child. All will be revealed."

With these words, the chaotic flailing of the corn stalks harmonised. The change was abrupt and alarming. As if brought about by the flick of a switch. I felt an irrepressible awe from the immense power of their unity. The true terror of what they can do to my body overwhelmed me for a moment. As visions of green stems snarling around my limbs flashed before my weary eyes, the plants spread open to reveal a path. I looked down the path to see something I thought I would never see again.

A door? Here? The curtain had come down on the uncanny dance of giant plants. They had fallen conspicuously still, as if terrified of disobeying the orders of an entity that was commanding them. The scratching on my scales soothed and the sickly smell began to fade. But in the deadly stillness of the vast room, I felt terrorised by the voice that brought these chaotic forces to the knee.

"Are you the one doing all this?" I yelled trying to sound self-assured.

The door flung open violently with a loud creak as if coming off its hinges.

"Come in!" The booming voice echoed with a jovial tone.

I approached the room with caution, glancing at the fibrous mounds of obedient corn stalks laying perfectly still all around me. I peeped through the door, my heart leaping out of my chest, only to see an ordinary living room. One I was shown by the custodians in film reels and pictures prepared to give us an idea of what normal Turkish family life looks like.

A large carpet with blood red petunias twisting and turning over intricate geometric shapes of cream and gold adorned the floor. The enraptured joy of the flowers, the only reminder of the lush life blooming right outside the door. A chandelier sporting faux candles that mimic flickering flames with electric light bulbs hung from the ceiling, laden with heavy chunks of crystal that reflected the light into tiny rainbows. A comfortable sofa with large floral patterns leaned against the wall invitingly.

Then I saw him...

An unusually corpulent man with an obscenely content look in his eyes. His plump chest and heavy arms defying the limits of the oversized suit meant to keep them contained. Overflowing from the seams of his dark trousers an insatiable rotund belly. And as the icing, a shiny top hat. Perhaps the only article of clothing on him that didn't seem to be on the brink of bursting apart, yielding to the hungry flesh of its wearer. Unmoved by my presence he continued arranging his toy trains on the tracks, winding them up or slowing them down. Pulling levers to change tracks, to close and open tiny bridges.

"Well bust my buffers!" he exclaimed with mock surprise. Without raising his eyes from the running trains.

"You seem like a busy man."

He laughed jovially "Indeed, indeed...Balancing the universe takes a lot of concentration."

"Where are my brothers? Where am I?" I yelled, against the sound of miniature trains blowing steam out of their tiny whistles.

"Interesting question. Where do you think you are?"

"Is all of this real? Is it all just a dream?"

"But aren't dreams real?"

I stuttered not knowing what to say. "Your brothers are in the same place as you are little turtle. I brought you here." He explained as if it made perfect sense. He pulled a small black dodecahedron between his thumb and index finger and held it against the faux-candle chandelier. Shutting one eye he inspected it against the light, turning it between his fingers.

"The Eye sees everything..." he muttered as if to reassure himself.

"Who are you?" I snapped back, losing my patience.

"You already know me, I already know you." He replied cryptically.

"If names matter, they know me as The Fat Controller..." He interrupted his sentence as if he had a better idea and picked up a diesel locomotive from a pile of toys. He gestured to it with an open hand:

"But you can call me, THE TURTLE TRAINER."

I caught a glint in his eye from underneath the brim of his dark hat. He winked at me with malicious playfulness...

"Get it?"

Nirvana Nectar
The grooviest taste

The Flavor of Eternal Harmony

You heard the word on the street? They say Nirvana Nectar is more than a drink. It's a groovy taste of something deeper, a sip that'll quiet the noise in your head. They say it opens doors... unlocks the mind... reveals what the squares don't want you to know.

Drop out and Tune Into a Different Frequency

Ditch the noise, the doubts, the useless thoughts cluttering your mind. Nirvana Nectar offers a different kind of clarity, a stillness that drowns out your own voice. Some call it peace, others call it... surrender.

Join Us Beneath the Lotus

Seek out Nirvana Nectar where shadows dance and eyes shine a little too bright. Eternal Harmony offers answers, a path, a purpose. All you gotta do is follow. So, bottoms up!

Nirvana Nectar
You HAVE TO try it!